Just a Bit of Fun

by

Robert Swindells

Coventry City Council	
WIL	
3 8002 02155 055 5	
Askews & Holts	Mar-2014
S TF	£5.99

First published in 2009 in Great Britain by
Barrington Stoke Ltd
18 Walker Street, Edinburgh, EH3 7LP

www.barringtonstoke.co.uk

ISBN: 978-1-84299-711-6

Printed in Great Britain by Bell & Bain Ltd

A Note from the Author

Once, a long time ago, when I was with the RAF in Germany, I had a scary thing happen to me. My mates and I were sitting round a ouija board. They say that's a way of talking to the dead. A ouija board has the letters of the alphabet round the edge, and a glass turned upside down in the middle of it. When you sit round the ouija board, you ask the spirits of the dead questions and the glass spells out the answers. They say the glass moves round the letters on the board without anyone pushing or steering it. That time when my friends and I were asking the ouija board questions, we asked who the spirit was that was moving the glass. The glass spelled out the word SHACK. That made us laugh because Shack was the nickname for a mate of ours who was on holiday in Norway. So, we thought, the ouija board thing must be rubbish. That proved it!

A few days later, police in Norway contacted us to say our friend Shack had drowned in a swimming accident. They told us the date when it happened, and it was a day or two before our experiment with the board. We were very shaken, and I for one have never touched a ouija board since.

Just a Bit of Fun doesn't have a ouija board in it, but it's about something else we maybe shouldn't mess with. See what you think.

For Big D and Pip:
friends more precious than they know.

Contents

Chapter 1
All Right For You

I'm Harley. That's my first name, and I bet you can guess my second. Go on – I'll give you three tries and you'll only need one.

Yes that's right – Davidson. Like the bike. My dad called me after a motorbike. Feel free to laugh, by the way. It's all right for you.

People always laugh. I don't care any more. I tell myself it could be worse: I could be called Honda Ninety or Yamaha One Two Five. *That'd* be worth laughing at.

I'm a boy, too. That's the other joke people have. They think Harley's a girl's name.

Anyway, I'm in Year Ten at Sorley Hill. It's Thursday afternoon – R.S. with Miss Lake. It's Halloween next week and Miss Lake's dead against Halloween. In the middle of the lesson, she starts slagging it off, same as every year.

"There's our world," she says, "and the spirit world. Demons dwell in the spirit world – unclean demons with evil plans who like nothing better than to creep into our world and spread their evil." She stops and waits a minute or so. She looks at us over her half-glasses. "We're lucky it's not that easy for them to reach us. They need a portal – a door-way between the worlds. But some of the things we humans do can open up such portals – things like gazing into crystal balls, trying to contact the dead and celebrating Halloween. Halloween is nothing but an excuse to make money. The shops make children think it's alright to do the sorts of things that open deathly portals and let dark forces invade our lives."

Dave Watson's hand goes up. Old Lake looks at him and he goes, "Bit over the top, Miss, don't you think? I mean, come on – Halloween's just a bit of fun, right? Doesn't hurt anyone. It's not like shooting smack or putting yourself on the outside of eight or nine vodkas."

It's no good, of course – nothing's going to change old Lake's mind. She's a fossil. Her brain is set in stone. Every year there's a Halloween Disco in the gym, and every year Miss Lake does her best to try and get it stopped. We all have a laugh at what Dave says, but all it does is set the teacher off again. The lesson drifts by and we don't learn anything new.

As for me, I can't wait for this year's Disco. There's something I've got to do that night.

Chapter 2
Uma Broom

There's this girl, Uma Broom. Daft name, nearly as daft as mine, but Uma's drop-dead gorgeous. She's in Year Eleven but I think she fancies me. Well, why not? Anyway, she'll be at the Disco, and I'm going as Count Dracula.

Yes, I *know*. A load of lads'll go as Drac, they always do. But they'll be nothing like as good as me. None of 'em, and I'll tell you why.

Last term, our drama teacher got some people from a dance company to come and work with a group of us at school. We had to do different sorts of exercises, mostly working

in pairs. Then they got us moving to music.
Dave Watson dropped out – said it was gay –
but the rest of us got well into it. We stopped
feeling embarrassed pretty quick. It wasn't
proper ballet – no tights or satin slippers, and
we didn't have to pretend to be flipping swans.
We wore trackies and trainers, and we did bits
out of *Dracula the Ballet*. I bet you didn't know
there *was* a ballet about Drac, did you? Well,
there is, and at the end of the course we
danced the best bits of it in front of the whole
school.

It was really great. Watson was gutted not
to be part of it. I saw the look on his face after
the show.

And here's the thing. I was Count Drac and
my costume was fab. It was made just for me
by someone who works for the dance group. I
got to keep it, too – because it wouldn't fit
anyone else. I even got to keep the black
patent shoes that went with it. So when I say
I'm going to the Disco as Count Dracula, I

mean I'm going as *Count Dracula*, not some sad plonker in a bin bag cloak and a plastic mask from the joke shop.

I was telling you about Uma Broom. The thing about Uma is, she's crazy about nice clothes. Fashion. For lads as well as girls. If you're one of those guys who dresses like his dad, you can forget being seen anywhere with Uma Broom. She wears cool stuff just to push the wheelie-bin out. And I know that when she sees me walking into the gym on Halloween, in my black cloak with the red silk inside and my pointy patent shoes, she'll flip.

And what I say is, bring it on.

Chapter 3
Having a Laugh

Have you got little sisters or brothers? If you have, you'll know what a pain they can be. I've got one of each. Ryan's ten and Meg's nine. And they're looking forward to Halloween. 'Course they are.

They're in primary school, so they don't have a Disco. They cut out witches in black paper and pumpkins in orange and stick 'em on class-room windows. They take pumpkins to school, too. Hollow 'em out and fix candles inside. Then they bring 'em home and put 'em by the door. And on Halloween night they want to go trick-or-treating, and *that's* where the pain comes in.

"Harley," goes Mum on Saturday tea-time. "Ryan and Meg'll want to go trick-or-treating on Wednesday."

"Uh – yeah," I grunt. I'm trying to catch the footie results on telly. "I know – they always do."

"The thing is, your dad and I aren't happy about kids their age out on the streets after dark."

"So don't let 'em go."

"*You* always loved trick-or-treating, Harley, and we never stopped *you*."

"No," I growl, "Dad used to shadow me and my mates like a spy. It was embarrassing."

"It was for your safety," says Mum, "and we want you to do the same for your sister and brother this year."

"*Me?*" I look at her. "Why me? What's wrong with Dad doing it?"

Mum frowns. "You're fifteen, Harley. It's time you started to help out with the little ones. They're to go to the houses on Park Villas, nowhere else. And you'll have them home by eight o'clock sharp."

"But Mum it's the *Disco* that night," I squeal. "It kicks off at seven. If I have the kids till eight I'm gonna miss half of it."

"What time does it finish?" says Mum.

"Ten."

"Well, if you get into your outfit before you take the children out, you'll be at the Disco by twenty past eight. That gives you an hour and forty minutes to dance, eat, do whatever. That's plenty of time."

I've missed all the footie results now. I shake my head. "Not doing it, Mum."

Mum looks at me. "Let's see what your father has to say about it when he gets in, shall we?"

I snort. I know what Dad'll have to say. *When you're working, bringing money into the house, you can please yourself some of the time. Until that day comes, you'll do as you're told and like it.*

Well, no, I *won't* like it. He can make me do stuff, but he can't make me like it.

What can I do? I can't believe I'll be missing the Disco. Maybe Ryan and Meg will take a bribe? They're in Meg's room, playing computer games. I knock and enter. "Hey, kids," I start.

"Get out, Harley," snarls Ryan, "can't you see we're busy?"

"Listen," I murmur. "It's Bonfire Night in under two weeks. Got plenty of money for fireworks, have you?"

Meg shakes her head. "No, but it's Halloween first. When we're out trick-or-treating, some people'll give us money as their treat. And we can give *that* to Dad to buy fireworks."

"Dream on," I say. "Most people *don't* give money. Most people give sweeties and stuff. I'll give you three quid each for fireworks, *if* ..."

"If *what?*" she asks. I can see she doesn't trust me.

"If you stay in Wednesday instead of trick-or-treating."

Ryan twists round on his chair. "Stay in on *Halloween?*" he hoots. "You're having a laugh, aren't you?"

I stay cool. "No, I'm serious. Three pounds. *Each*. You won't get *that* knocking on doors."

"We'll take the chance," he growls. "Shut the door when you leave, big bro."

What can you do?

Chapter 4

Toffee Monsters

One thing you can do is up your offer.
I try, Sunday morning. "Four," I hiss across the
breakfast table. Dad's gone out to wash the
car. Mum's cleaning up. "Four pounds each,
how about it?"

"Pathetic, Harley," murmurs Ryan. "One
rocket costs three quid. We'd get, like, two
fireworks each for missing Halloween. That's
rubbish."

"Five," I cry. "Final offer."

"Stuff it," grates my sweet little sister. So I know I've got no hope.

So here we are, the three of us, seven o'clock Wednesday, dolled up ready to go. Dad's giving me the eye. He's like, "Think on, Harley. Park Villas only. They're not to step off the pavement, let alone cross the road. And don't let them out of your sight, not for a second. If anyone invites them indoors, you go in with them. You never know what goes on in other people's houses."

This is totally over the top. Park Villas is all piano teachers and other old people. How'd they harm anyone? They're too busy saving the whale. But it's no use arguing. "It'll be fine, Dad," I mutter. "Let's go, monsters."

We set off. It's a damp, misty evening. Ryan's dressed up as a skeleton. He's got a black suit with greenish glow-in-the-dark bones on it and a hood. Meg's a witch in rags and a pointy hat. Her eyes glitter as she peeps through the holes in a stiff green mask. She's excited. "You both look stupid," I tell them. What I want is to be at the gym with Uma Broom. So why should I be nice? If any of my mates clock me baby-sitting I'll have to kill myself.

There's only one side to Park Villas. It's a long line of gloomy old houses. The bay windows still look out over Jenner Park. No one can build there because rich Mr Jenner – who was an inventor or something – left it forever to the people of Sorley. We stop at house Number One. There's no gate, just a short, damp path and two steps up to the door.

"Go on, then," I say. "What're you waiting for?"

Meg shivers. "Dunno, Harley. It's always scary, the first one."

"Yeah, well." I give a shrug. "They *do* say the woman who lives here's mad."

"*Mad?*" gulps Meg.

"As a hatter. She used to teach music, but she murdered a pupil and hid the body inside the piano. The blind man who came to tune the piano found it."

"Oooh!" Meg shudders. "I'm not knocking *here*, then."

"Don't be such a wimp," growls Ryan. "Can't you see Harley's just trying to spoil it for us? He didn't want to bring us out."

I try my Count Dracula voice. "Go right ahead, young sir – the lady and I will follow you."

He goes up the path first, I'll give him that. Of course, I've made it all up. I know that an old guy lives here by himself. Meg hangs back till she sees the old man open the door. I lurk behind the hedge so no one sees me. What sort of loser goes trick-or-treating when they're *fifteen*, for God's sake?"

The old guy's really into it. He cries out when he sees Meg and Ryan, then shakes with fake fear as he backs along the hall-way to get them a treat. Never grow up, some people. I turn my back and stare across the road at the jungle of trees by the park wall.

And that's when I first see the white thing, fluttering. It's half-hidden among the trees so that I can't see it very well. *Could be a plastic bag*, I tell myself, *stuck on a branch, flapping in the wind.*

What wind? There's isn't any wind. It wouldn't be misty if there was. But the white bag *is* fluttering about in the trees. *Something's* making it move. Or maybe it's a barn owl – I think *they're* white. Doesn't look much like a barn owl. More like a flag. A raggy white flag.

"*Wake up, Harley!*" It's Ryan, but I damn near jump out of my skin. "What's up?" he says.

17

"N ... nothing." I shake my head. "It's nothing. What did you get?"

"All these." He opens the bag on his belt. It's crammed with toffees. "Meg's got just as many."

"Huh!" I grunt. "You can't buy fireworks with toffees, can you?"

"Plenty more houses," chirps Meg. "Come on."

I look across the road again, quickly. I can't see anything white. I trot after the toffee monsters.

Chapter 5
A Trick of the Light

"Trick or treat?"

"I'll trick or treat *you*, you little monkeys. Clear off before I let the dog out."

We're at Number Two. The *kids* are – I'm waiting by the gate. Number Two does have a gate. When the woman starts yelling I shove it open and walk up her path.

"That's my brother and sister you're bawling at, you sad old cow," I snarl. She looks at me like I'm something the cat coughed up.

"Get out of my garden this instant, and take your brother and sister with you, or I'll call the police."

"You must be one of those sad oldies who were never young themselves," I hiss in her face. She steps back, slams the door in mine. "Come on, kids," I snap. "Idiots like her aren't worth bothering with."

"At least she didn't set the dog on us," says Meg as we get back to the street.

"I bet she hasn't even *got* a dog," says Ryan. "Why don't we dream up a really bad trick to play on her."

"No way!" I grab their hands and we walk away. "Like I said, she's not worth the bother. Better luck at Number Three, eh?"

Meg peers up the path. "C ... come with us, Harley," she murmurs.

I shake my head. "No, but I'll tell you what – my offer's still open. You can take that four

quid each and I'll get you home safe right now
if you want."

"It was *five* quid," growls Ryan, "and you
can keep it. C'mon, Meg." He takes her hand
and they set off down the next garden. This
one's full of big bushes. I sit on the low wall to
wait.

It's there again, just opposite. Fluttering.
We've moved, and the thing's moved with us.
Weird. I look hard into the mist but I can't
make out what it is. I hear the kids knock and
the door open. "Trick or treat," pipes Ryan.
No yell follows, so that's all right. I get up,
walk to the pavement edge, peer across.

It isn't a flag, it's not the right shape. It
doesn't have a proper shape. It's like
someone's waving a bit of white silk in the air,
making swirly patterns. Except no one's there.
The thing's moving all by itself, in the black
under the trees.

This time when we move on, I keep my head turned to the right so I can watch it. I tell myself it can't *really* have followed us. It must be my eyes or a trick of the light – an optical illusion. But I don't feel like turning my back on it.

"We got a pound each," crows Ryan. "Soon beat your stupid fiver now, Harley."

"Right," I say. "Good." I'm not really listening to him. We're at the gate to Number Four, and the thing's still level with us. "Go on, then," I croak. "Off you pop." I can't let the kids see I'm scared, 'cos I'm not. I just want to know what the thing is, that's all.

Meg and Ryan go off up the path, all giggles. They're having fun now, not nervous at all. Well, they've got their big brother backing them up, haven't they? They don't know their back-up's getting spooked by a rag on a twig.

I stand and stare across at the trees, at the park, at the white thing. A car swishes past. Did the driver notice it? Even if he *did*, it'd be no big deal. It's a torn bag, for God's sake. "You're a bit of litter," I murmur. "That's all *you* are."

Am I going mad – *talking to litter?*

"Hell-*o*, Harley, we're *done* here." I turn and stick a grin on my face. Meg's grinning too. "More money," she tells me. "Best Halloween ever."

I nod. "That's good, Meg. You two carry on with Number Five, I'll be with you in a sec."

Ryan stares at me through his skull hood. "Is something wrong, Harley?"

"No, no." I shake my head. "Everything's cool, Ryan. I'm crossing the road for a minute, that's all. Don't follow or you'll get me in trouble. Do Number Five, wait for me outside Six, OK?"

Ryan gives a shrug. "Right, Drac. Come on, Meg."

I don't *want* to cross. Don't want to be any closer to that thing than I am now, but that's stupid. I'm letting my fear make a prat out of me. Because that's all it is – fear. I'm going to show it who's boss. No one makes a prat out of *me*.

A truck's coming. I let it pass, hope the white thing vanishes after the truck's gone. It doesn't. I start to cross the road, my eyes fixed every second on that scrap of white. As I get to the other side, something shifts in my head and what I see now is different. It's like when you stare at that trick picture and it stops being two black faces and turns into a white vase. The white plastic bag's gone. Now I can see a girl standing among the trees. A girl in a white dress. I don't know why I didn't see her before. The moon breaks through and pours soft light on the girl's face and my heart

kicks me in the ribs. The girl is Uma Broom.
And she's smiling at me.

Chapter 6
A Bit Undead

"Uma, *hey!*" I gawp. My heart's thumping. "Why're you ... I mean, what are you *doing* here, what about the Disco?"

I've lost it totally, I'm talking rubbish. It's the shock. It doesn't fit. Why is Uma here?

Uma says nothing, just stands there smiling. Maybe she missed me at the Disco, came looking for me. But that's crap. It doesn't make sense. A girl like Uma can have any guy she wants. Why would she leave the Disco for *me?* And anyway, how did she know where I was?

A horrible thought makes me go hot all over. *She's come for a laugh. Somehow, she found out I was baby-sitting in my Count Dracula kit, and she's here to mock. There's maybe half the kids in my year behind those trees, peeing themselves laughing.*

"Come for a giggle, have you, Uma?" I snarl. "You and the others? Well, go on then – laugh. See if *I* care." I *do* care, but no way am I going to let Uma see that. I'm turning away and she laughs, but it isn't a mocking laugh. It's the sing-song laugh she uses with her friends – the laugh that melts my bones when I hear it at school. I've got to *do* something so I swing myself over the wall. If Uma Broom wants me to join her in Jenner Park, I'm not complaining.

I get up close to her, can't believe my luck. When I can nearly reach out and touch her, she turns and runs off between the trees, still laughing. Something tells me she's not running to get away from me, but to tease. "Here I *come*," I shout, "ready or not." If Uma wants to play chase, that's OK with me. In fact, it's a great idea.

She's out of the trees now and she jogs onto the footy field. The white dress soaks up moonlight. She has on those little silver shoes. They must be all messed up with mud and wet grass. She's still laughing, like little bells ringing.

On grass I run fast. I need to catch her and ask her what she's playing at, but I seem to be getting no closer. "Uma!" I pant. I feel like a wimp. "Hang on a minute, I want to tell you something."

She looks back and slows down a bit. The gap between us gets smaller. The pond's just in front of her, she'll have to stop now. "Uma," I gasp, "we're missing the Disco. How about if you and me ...?"

The words die away as I say them. Uma's at the pond, but she doesn't stop. The moon has made a silvery path across the water.

Without waiting a moment, she's on it. I croak a warning but there's no splash. She jogs out across the bright surface of the pond, and *now* her laughter mocks me as I stand frozen and watching.

Some guy wrote graffiti on the bog wall at school – *Uma Broom walks on water.* But that's just what guys say about someone who's cool. No one *really* walks on water. No one. And yet ...

You've *got* to believe what you see, haven't you? And there's Uma, out in the middle of the pond, dancing and laughing, swirling that beautiful dress. As I stare with my mouth open, some words of Miss Lake's come back to me. ... *unclean demons with evil plans* ...

"*It isn't HER, you plank!*" screeches a voice inside my skull. "*That's not Uma Broom. It isn't a person at all. It's a ...*"

Yes, I *know* how daft it sounds, and I know exactly what you're thinking. You're thinking,

He's flipped his lid, fallen out of his tree. He'll be telling us next she got on her broomstick and flew away. He'll say that's why she's called Broom.

Well, you can think what you like – you weren't there. I was, and I know what I *saw*. I stand and watch *her* or *it* or whatever, dancing on the top of the pond. It's for real – right in front of my eyes, and I'm so busy staring that it takes a minute or two before I remember what I'm meant to be doing.

The kids – I'm meant to be looking after the kids. *Don't let 'em out of your sight*, said Dad, *even for a second*. And where are they now? Hundreds of metres away. I wouldn't hear if they shouted, or know if they got run over by a truck. I've let this girl – this thing that *looks* like a girl – take me away from my brother and sister. And there's me saying, *No one makes a prat out of me*. Well, *she* has, hasn't she? And that's *nothing* to what Dad'll make out of me if anything's happened to the kids.

The thought of Dad when he's angry scares me into looking away from that weird dance on the water, or I swear I'd be standing there yet. As it is, I start running back across the footy field – I don't even look back. Thinking about what I'd see if I *did* look back makes me run even faster. I sprint back to Park Villas and I'm fretting all the way.

How long have I been in the park? Five minutes? Ten? I haven't a clue, it's as if time stopped the second I saw Uma – if it was Uma. That thing took over my brain, drove out everything else. Now I feel as if I'm in a dream as I fly gasping over the muddy turf.

Then I'm under the trees. I can see the street-lamps, the road. *Why?* screams a voice in my head. *Why did that thing lead me away? What did it want with me?* Deep down I *know*, of course I do. It was one of Miss Lake's *unclean demons*, and it led me off so that its mates could get a crack at Meg and Ryan.

31

Twigs and branches pluck and rip at my clothes, but I don't care. I get over the wall and scan the houses. No one's waiting outside Number Six, or Seven, or Eight. Cold fear floods my guts. I dash across the road without looking. If anything's coming I'm dead but I don't care. I blunder up the path of Number Five and hammer on the door. "Come *ON*!" I screech. "Are you all flipping deaf or what?"

I'm about to give the door a kick when it cracks open. A guy in glasses blinks through the gap. He looks like an owl in a hollow tree. "What's your problem, Dracula?" he asks. "Don't you think you're a bit too old to be trick-or-treating? A bit ... er ... *undead?*"

Chapter 7
Where's Your Dog?

I blurt out, "I ... I'm *not* trick-or-treating, I've lost two kids. Did they knock here?"

He nods, calm. "A witch and a skeleton. We gave them a pound or two and they left."

"How long?" I ask.

"Huh?"

"How long *ago?*" I ask again.

"About ten minutes. I heard them knock next door."

"Number Six, yeah?"

"That's right. Mr and Mrs White. They're all right."

All right? I nod. "Thanks, I'll try there."

"Good luck. Call back if there's anything I can do."

They're not at Number Six now, unless they're inside. I ring the bell. I see a light go on somewhere. I'm like, "Come *on*, for God's sake." I hop from foot to foot and look across at the black trees in the park.

A woman opens the door. "Two kids," I pant, "are they here?"

"Kids? You mean the trick-or-treaters?" She shakes her head. "They ran away before I'd a chance to give them their treat. We'd never invite children in anyway."

"They ran?" I don't understand.

"Yes," the woman says.

"Which way?" I ask.

"I don't know, dear, I didn't stay to watch. Are they missing?"

"Yes, they just seem to have ... vanished," I say.

"I'm sorry, young man. You're welcome to come in and use the phone if you wish."

"The *phone?*" I don't see how that would help.

"Yes, to call the police," the woman tries to tell me.

"Oh, no, that's fine, I've got my moby. I hope I don't have to ring the *police*."

The woman smiles. "I forget people have mobys." She frowns. "Do the *children* have one?"

I shake my head. "Not tonight. But that's a good thought – thanks." I turn and hurry down the path.

35

She calls after me, "Children almost always turn up safe and sound, you know."

Almost is a dangerous word.

I look down Park Villas. A black cat is sniffing at the foot of a street-lamp. A car speeds by, music thudding out. Across the road, way down, an old man is walking his dog in the shadows of the trees. *I don't half wish I was you*, I think, *or the guy in that car. Someone who hasn't lost kids, who doesn't know what's dancing and laughing out there in the park tonight. In fact, I'd rather be your dog than me.*

At least if I was a dog I wouldn't have to face Mum and Dad.

My brain's shut down. I'm in a sort of dream, doing nothing but gawp. I haven't a clue how long I stand gazing down the road, but I'm jerked out of it by a crash of splintering glass. Then there's a scream, then wild laughter. *Children's* laughter.

It's coming from Number Two. What was it Ryan said – *Why don't we dream up a really bad trick to play on her?* "No!" I yell. "For God's sake, *no*. RYAN! Meg!" I pelt back to Number Two, shouting like a madman.

The gate's open. I brake, swerve through the gate, dash up the path and stop dead. It's worse than I expected – *much* worse. The middle bay window is smashed. There's a drift of glittering bits of glass on the sill, and sharp glass teeth jut out of the window frame. The house door is open. The woman is standing on the step, her arms up in front of her face. Dark, sticky stuff is smeared all over her hands, knees and hair. Meg and Ryan have got their backs to me and they're throwing handfuls of small stones at her and chanting, "Where's your dog? Where's your dog? Where's your dog?"

Everything happens at once. Fast foot-steps behind me and someone gasps, "My God, oh, my God!" A guy with white hair grabs my

sleeve. He's the man who lives at Number
Three. "Miss Conrad," he croaks, "wh … what
on *earth* are you doing to Miss Conrad?"
Before I can reply another guy comes up the
path. "I heard glass," he wheezes, "is
something the matter?" He's the old chap from
Number One. He peers at what's going on in
the garden and gasps. "They're *murdering*
her!" he cries. "Stop them, someone call the
police."

Both men turn on me. "*You* put 'em up to
this, you *must* have. Stop them right now, or
we *will*." They look nasty. They're angry and
their faces look mean. I dash up to the door.
"Meg, Ryan," I shouted as I grab them, "what
the heck d'you think you're *doing?*" I swing
them round, shake them as hard as I can.
"Can't you see you're *killing* the lady. They'll
put you in prison."

Meg pushes her face up to mine. She looks
totally different. Her face is so twisted. I feel
as if don't know my sister at all. "Why do *you*

care, Harley?" she snarls through her teeth.
"You *said* she's not worth bothering with, so let
go of me before I rip your face off." She's
taken her mask off but her eyes are empty and
ugly. I jerk my head away from her but not
fast enough. A hand flashes out and claws like
hooks rip into my cheek. It hurts. I let go of
Meg as I clap my hand to my face. She skips
away from me and spits like a cat. And I
suddenly know with a cold shock it isn't Meg at
all.

Ryan twists free too. He joins his sister on
the lawn. The chanting starts again. "Where's
your dog? Where's your dog? Where's your
dog?" They point their fingers at Miss Conrad
and mock her. They stab the air in time with
the chant.

All this time the woman's trying to get
back in the house. Her hand's feeling for the
door but she daren't take her eyes off the kids.
I move up to the door so I'm standing between
her and them. There's a really bad smell – the

gunk on her is dog shit. There's more on the step, on the door-knob and the letter slot. I reach out. What I want to do is help her back inside.

"Don't touch me!" she shouts and jerks her arm away. "Don't you *dare* lay hands on me." She starts to back towards the open door. "What sort of people *are* you? Where do you *live?* Look what the children have done to my house."

I look at her and then back at Meg and Ryan. I shake my head. "I ... don't think it's children we're dealing with," I croak.

"Don't think it's children we're dealing with," Ryan chants in a silly voice.

"... Children we're dealing with," screeches Meg. The two of them burst into laughter and skip round the lawn.

Chapter 8
Aliens?

The woman shakes with a mixture of fear and anger. "This is too much. I'm ringing the police right now," she chokes. The man who lives at Number One's come up to the door. "Yes – we need the police here right now," he growls. "Assault and battery, criminal damage – this is a police matter, all right." He grabs my arm. He's not strong, and he's so old that I could knock him down easily. But I don't. I *so* don't want the police involved.

It's then that I see the other guy has his moby out. *Does he have pictures of the kids?* I think. *Of me, of the damage?* Photo evidence. Now he's punching a number into the phone. I shout out to him, "What you doing?"

"What d'you *think* I'm doing?" he snorts. "Calling the police, of course."

"No, wait," I beg. *"Please.* We're not people like this, I promise. We live on Grasmere Drive. The kids've never been in trouble, and neither have I. Our dad's in charge of security down at the Shopping Centre. He could lose his job if ..."

The woman glares at me. "Your sister and brother should have thought of that before they smashed my window, smeared dog dirt all over my step. Before they threw stones at me to *kill* me."

I shake my head. "Not to kill you," I gibber. I'm so scared I don't know what I'm saying. "They're little, they don't understand, they only meant to play a trick on you ..."

"A *trick?*" She looks down at herself and at her filthy hands, then over at the smashed window. "You call this a trick? It isn't a trick, it's a wicked assault. Normal people don't deserve to be attacked in their own homes like this, it's totally wrong."

I nod. I'm scared spitless, but I see that the old man from Number Three is listening. He hasn't put in his call yet. "I *know,*" I tell her. "You're right, but you see ..." I stop and take a deep breath. "This is going to sound daft, but I think something's taken them over."

"What – like *aliens,* you mean?" The woman snorts. "You've the nerve to stand there and tell me that that pair of little things are aliens from ... from where – *Mars?*"

I shake my head. "N ... no, not aliens. It's Halloween, you see. Our R.S. teacher reckons that at Halloween things ... *portals,* open up between the spirit world and this one, and unclean demons come into our world. I didn't

43

believe her, but now ..." I nod at Ryan and Meg, who are standing still and silent on the lawn. "I think it could be true, because I've never seen my brother and sister act like this. In fact, they don't even *look* like my sister and brother. Their eyes ..."

"This is all rubbish," growls the man from house Number Three. "Let's stop messing about and get the police here." He looks at me. "Try telling the cops these kids have demons in them, see where it gets you."

"Wait, please, Arthur." Miss Conrad holds up a hand. Number Three gives a sigh and puts his moby down again. She looks at me. "Where do you go to school, young man?"

"Sorley Hill."

"You're talking about Mildred Lake, then?"

"Yes, that's right." I feel a flicker of hope. "D'you know her?"

The woman nods. "We were at college together." She looks towards the lawn where Meg and Ryan, silent now, stand watching us. "She talks a lot of sense, does Mildred Lake. Always did." She shivers. "And she might well be right about 'unclean demons'. I've never liked Halloween, which is why I don't like trick-or-treating."

"Well, *I've* always loved it," I tell her, "but I'm not so sure now. Listen," I look at her, "I promise I'll clean everything up, and I know my dad'll pay for the window, only please don't get the police."

The woman isn't sure. "Well, I don't know …" She shows me her hands, points with a foot at the filthy step. "All this. My window. It's all most upsetting. The mocking, the stones. I shouldn't have to …"

"I *know*, you're right." I take out my moby. "Look, I'm phoning my dad. He'll be gutted when I tell him what's happened, he'll come

45

right away. We're not a family of vandals, Miss Conrad."

Miss Conrad doesn't seem sure. I wait. I hope the two old men will give me a chance – that they won't ring the police for her. I'm looking at the kids as well – one more taunt, another chant, and we're stuffed. We all stand silent and wait for Mrs Conrad to tell us what she's going to do.

This silence goes on a long time. I picture what would happen if the police call at our place and tell Dad his kids have attacked an old woman with stones and smashed up her house. He'll love that, and he'll admire the hell out of me for the great job I've done looking after the kids.

Not.

After about six million years, Miss Conrad speaks. "Phone your father if you wish," she murmurs, "but I don't want *anyone* to see me like this. He must come tomorrow if he wishes to talk to me."

She turns to her two neighbours. "Thank you, Arthur, and you, Neil, for coming to my rescue. My attackers might have been hulking brutes, not children, in which case you'd have been in some danger yourselves. I'm grateful to you both." She doesn't look at me or the kids, but goes in and closes the door.

The old men look at me and then at each other. Arthur's like, "You're luckier than you deserve, lad. You can thank your lucky stars our Miss Conrad was at college with your Miss Lake, because that's what swung it." I watch the pair shuffle away down Miss Conrad's path, then I walk over to the kids. Their eyes look normal now, that awful emptiness has gone.

"Meg, Ryan, I'm phoning home. I don't know what got into you both while I was gone, but it's my fault. I should never have left you. Are you feeling all right now?"

They nod. They both look worn out. "*I* don't know what it was either, Harley," murmurs Meg, "but I felt it go from me. It was when Miss Conrad said '*she might well be right about unclean demons*'. It was as if something flew off me. It had been *found out*, you see, so it ran away." She frowns. "Does that make sense?"

I nod. "Perfect sense, Meg. Maybe it thought we'd fetch someone to get rid of it – you know, *cast it out?* Maybe it hurts, being cast out."

Ryan's staring at the smashed window. "We wouldn't dare do stuff like that," he murmurs, "but we *did*, didn't we, Harley?"

I nod. "You did, Ryan, sort of, but it wasn't really you." I look at him. "Did you feel *yours* run away?"

He frowns. "Maybe, I don't know. I felt scared, and ... angry, I think."

48

"That was *it*, Ryan – the demon. *It* was scared and angry, not you. So it ran away."

"I ... picked up *dog poo*," whispers Meg, "with my *hands*." She's rubbing them on her witch's skirt. "They *stink*. I think I'm going to be sick."

And she throws up in the middle of Miss Conrad's lawn.

I call home, tell Dad there's been a bit of trouble, say he'd better come and look. He's there in four minutes. Mum's with him.

I won't bang on about it. He *is* gutted. They both are. Dad fetches rags and spirit from the car. I help him clean up Miss Conrad's door-handle and letter slot. It's too dark to do much about the step. Dad scrawls a note and shoves it through the slot.

Dear Miss Conrad,

We're so, so sorry. I'll be back in the morning to set things right. I'll have my

49

cheque-book with me. Thanks for taking it so well.

Tom Davidson.

By this time Meg and Ryan are in floods of tears. The shock's gone and the full horror of what's happened is sinking in.   To tell you the truth, I'm not feeling too great myself. We pile into the car and Dad drives us home. The Disco has half an hour to run, but my outfit's a mess now and anyway, me and Halloween are finished. I go to bed the same as Meg and Ryan, but I can't sleep.

Chapter 9
Stuff We Can't Explain

Next morning it's the first of November. The stuff that happened last night seems like a dream to me. I think Meg and Ryan feel the same.

But it wasn't a dream. Dad's already at Park Villas. He's kept his promise to Miss Conrad. I can tell that Mum's bursting to ask the kids about it all, but she doesn't. She lets them miss school, they're still worn out and very upset.

I've said it was all my fault. "I saw something," I say, "under the trees in the park." I don't say much more. "It drew me away, I forgot all about Meg and Ryan. Something got to them while I was gone. I'm really sorry."

I mean it.

But I *do* have to go to school. Mum's like, "You'll be dying to know how the Disco went. And your friends will *really* want to know what happened to you."

Yeah, right. Like I'm gonna tell 'em I spent Halloween baby-sitting. How uncool is that! Mums just don't get it.

I get to school at 8.30. First guy I see is Dave Watson. "Davidson!" he booms, so everyone can hear. "Where were *you* last night, dude, you missed the best Disco ever."

I shrug. "Not bothered, Watson."

He looks at me. "Not *bothered?* I thought you couldn't wait to boogie into the gym in your ultra-cool Dracula kit?"

I pull a face. "Well, yeah – I have to admit I was looking forward to running it by Uma Broom, see if it'd make her fancy me."

Watson shakes his head. "Wouldn't have happened anyway, mate – she didn't show up either."

Weird, or what? And no – it *can't* have been her in the park – I'm not saying that. But stuff happens, doesn't it, sometimes? Stuff we can't explain.

Two things I know. One – Miss Lake's not the sad old fossil I took her for. And two – I go cold every time I hear that sing-song laugh I heard in Jenner Park.

Barrington Stoke would like to thank all its readers for commenting on the manuscript before publication and in particular:

June Authbert
Gemma Backhouse
Jayde Beardshall
Thomas Braithwaite
Reece Buck
Jack Campbell
Andrew Cavanagh
Vicky Cook
Shona Cosgrove
Hayden Dayvies
Beth Derlin
Shonagh Donegan
James Ellis
Robert Featherstone
George Hickes
Rachel Hughes
Andrew Humphrey
Eimhear Jackson

Lewis Jackson
Chelsea Kettlewell
Jenny Linsley
Chantelle Magson
Rebecca McAllister
Caitlynde McAree
Deirdre McConnell
Shannon Molowy
Mr Newman
Tom Oliver
Naomi O'Reilly
Nicole Pearson
Michaela Quinn
Nicole Ryan
Danny Thointon
Sue Tomlinson
Jake Wilstron

Become a Consultant!

Would you like to give us feedback on our titles before they are published? Contact us at the email address below – we'd love to hear from you!

info@barringtonstoke.co.uk
www.barringtonstoke.co.uk

The First Hunter

Tan and his people steal meat from the big cats to live. It's dangerous. It's scary.
Wid the Fool thinks there's a better way. Could they hunt like cats, not steal like jackals?
But no one listens to Wid. Until now.

Burnout

One spark was all it took. He was hooked from the first flame.
Now, when Josh starts fires, nothing else matters. It's just him. The moment. The power.
But like they say, if you play with fire, someone's going to get burned ...

You can order these books directly from our website at
www.barringtonstoke.co.uk

Also by Robert Swindells

Snakebite

Snake in the grass ...
Mark is the boss on the
estate. He thinks Alex
grassed him up. Mark isn't
happy.
Now Alex is hunted,
trapped – and on his own.
After all, Mark is the boss,
and Alex is a loser with
only a pet snake to talk to.
Get out of that one, Snake
Boy ...

Knife-Edge

Cecil True's gang runs
Sam's estate. They beat
kids up, nick their stuff.
Sam's scared he's next.
That's why he steals the
commando knife. When he
carries the knife, Sam thinks
he's safe. He thinks he's
hard. He thinks he can take
on Cecil True.
Sam's wrong.

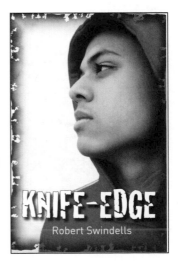

You can order these books directly from our website at
www.barringtonstoke.co.uk